RIP VAN WINKLE

RIP VAN WINKLE

RETOLD AND ILLUSTRATED BY
WILL MOSES
FROM THE ORIGINAL STORY BY
WASHINGTON IRVING

PHILOMEL BOOKS
NEW YORK

Patricia Lee Gauch, editor

Copyright © 1999 by Will Moses. All rights reserved. This book, or parts thereof,
may not be reproduced in any form without permission in writing from the publisher,
Philomel Books, a division of Penguin Putnam Books for Young Readers ,
345 Hudson Street, New York, NY 10014.
Philomel Books, Reg. U.S. Pat. & Tm. Off. Published simultaneously in Canada.
Printed in Hong Kong by South China Printing Co. (1988) Ltd.
Book design by Gunta Alexander. The text is set in Trump Mediaeval.

The art was done in oil on Fabriano paper.

Library of Congress Cataloging-in-Publication Data
Moses, Will. Rip Van Winkle / retold and illustrated by Will Moses
from the original story by Washington Irving. p. cm.
Summary: A retelling of the tale in which a man who sleeps for twenty years in the
Catskill Mountains wakes to a much-changed world. [1. Catskill Mountains Region (N.Y.)—
Fiction. 2. New York (State)—Fiction] I. Irving, Washington, 1783-1859. Rip Van Winkle.
II. Title PZ7.M8477Ri 1999 [Fic]—dc21   97-39929 CIP AC   ISBN 0-399-23152-8
1 3 5 7 9 10 8 6 4 2
First Impression

For Moo & Zippy

Thanks!

AUTHOR'S NOTE

In every town there resides a Rip Van Winkle. A Dame Van Winkle. And many of the others from the cast of characters who make this story happen. The genius of Washington Irving is that his larger-than-life stories revolve around characters we have all known in our own lives. Oddly, while we imagine how much we have changed in the two hundred years since Rip roamed the Catskill Mountains, I think it is the fact that we see so much of ourselves in Rip and his companions that endears them to us, even today.

Washington Irving's stories are among America's greatest literary treasures. The opportunity to retell and illustrate two of his most-loved tales, *The Legend of Sleepy Hollow* and *Rip Van Winkle*, has been a tremendous honor and great joy. Irving's characters and words seem to lend themselves to the stories I try to create with my art. When I paint his stories, I always feel as if I am part of the world he has created. All the details become real to me. It is my hope that each person uses his imagination to visually enter this world and create his own personal story within.

I have retold and illustrated this rendition of *Rip Van Winkle* with both the young-in-body and young-at-heart in mind. I hope it will be a storybook for families to enjoy for years to come.

Will Moses

Whoever has made a voyage up the Hudson River must remember the Catskill Mountains, rising magnificently to the west of it. Swelling up to noble heights, they change appearance, not only with every season but with each change of the weather as well. Indeed, it seems every hour of the day brings with it some magical transformation to the colors and shapes of these old mountains.

Lying at the foot of those fairy mountains called the Catskills, snugly nestled among the trees and fresh green meadows, the voyager may remember a peculiar and ancient village. It is here, in this hamlet of great antiquity, first settled by some of the earliest Dutch explorers, that my story takes place. For it was here that there lived a simple, good-natured fellow, by the name of Rip Van Winkle.

Rip was a kind man and a friendly neighbor. Above all else, he was a free spirit, who, in spite of his wife's regular encouragement, managed to avoid all labor! Dame Van Winkle, quite the opposite, was energetic and full of ambition, a hard worker and always eager to get a job done. Certainly these were noble qualities, but as the whole village knew too well, Dame Van Winkle also was remarkable for her surly disposition, which could be matched only by her savage temper. Unfortunately for poor Rip, he was the most frequent target of his wife's scorn. For Rip's laziness made her blood boil!

Most of the villagers, having experienced Dame Van Winkle's hot temper at one time or another, had abundant sympathy for Rip. Indeed, most of his neighbors easily overlooked his bad habits and took him for who he was: good-natured, agreeable, happy-go-lucky Rip Van Winkle. The children of the village especially enjoyed him, shouting with joy whenever he approached.

Rip often assisted with their sports and helped make their playthings. He spent hours on end teaching them to fly kites and shoot marbles, and telling long stories of ghosts, witches, and Indians. Frequently he was sur-rounded by a troop of children, hanging on his coattails, clambering on his back, or playing tricks on him. In fact, so great was Rip's popularity, not even dogs barked at him as he made his rounds throughout the town!

Rip's chief flaw, of course, was his dislike for all work. This was not from an inability to persevere, for he would sit on a wet rock with a long heavy pole in hand, fishing all day without a complaint and often without having so much as a nibble. And he frequently could be seen carrying his big shotgun on his shoulder, trudging through woods and swamps and over hill and dale, only to shoot a few tired squirrels or wild pigeons.

Never would he refuse to help a neighbor, and he was absolutely the foremost man at all country frolics and games. The women of the village, too, found him eager to do the little odd jobs their less obliging husbands would not. In a word, Rip was always ready to attend to anybody's business but his own. When it came to keeping his own farmstead in order, he found it impos-sible. His fences were constantly falling to pieces, and his cow would either go astray or, worse, graze upon his cabbages.

Weeds grew quicker and thicker in his fields than anywhere else, and rain always made a point of setting in just as he had some outdoor work to do. So, under Rip's care, the Van Winkle farm dwindled away, acre by acre, until there was little more than a sparse field of Indian corn and a scant patch of potatoes.

Rip's children too were as ragged and wild as if they belonged to nobody! His son, Rip, promised to inherit all the bad traits of the father. He was often seen trotting like a colt at his mother's heels, outfitted in a pair of his

father's cast-off boots, which were too big and flew off his feet whenever he ran, or stepped in mud.

Old Rip Van Winkle, however, was one of those happy mortals who take the world easy, eat white bread or brown, and would rather starve on a penny than work for a pound. If left alone, he would whistle life away in a perfect haze of contentment.

Morning, noon, and night his wife kept a ringing in his ears, harping continually on his idleness, his carelessness, and the ruin he was bringing upon his family. Rip had but one way of replying to her tongue-lashings: he shrugged his shoulders, shook his head, cast up his big eyes, and said nothing, enraging her even more.

Rip's one true friend and companion was his faithful dog, Wolf. Unfortunately for poor Wolf, Dame Van Winkle regarded him as Rip's companion in idleness, believing him to be the main cause of her husband's so often going astray. In truth, though, Wolf was as good and courageous a dog as ever roamed the woods. Brave as he was, Wolf, not unlike his master, frequently withered under the scouring of Dame Van Winkle's temper.

As time went by, Rip found himself escaping the farmstead more and more in order to avoid Dame

Van Winkle and to escape from the work he knew to be of no use anyway!

On these occasions he would console himself by keeping company with the sages, philosophers, and other idlers from the village, who gathered daily before a small inn (which in those pre-Revolutionary days distinguished itself with a sign bearing a portrait of King George III). Here, before the inn, this band of thinkers and loafers wasted away the long, lazy days of summer, doing little more than discussing village gossip or telling endless sleepy stories about nothing. Occasionally an old newspaper would fall their way, and Derrick Van Bummel, the schoolmaster, would read aloud the news accounts. Of course, these stories were just fodder for more talk! Oddly, none of the men seemed to mind in the least, that most stories from the paper had occurred months earlier and had probably long since been resolved!

The ringleader of this customary gathering was Nicholas Vedder, landlord of the inn. Seated from morning to night near the doorway of the inn, he barely moved, except to avoid the sun and to keep in the shade of a large tree. Vedder rarely spoke his opinions aloud, but as he smoked his pipe ceaselessly, his followers were able to understand him perfectly. When anything was read or discussed that displeased him, he was observed to smoke his pipe vehemently, sending forth short, frequent, angry puffs.

Even from this friendly stronghold, the unlucky Rip was, after a time, routed. Dame Van Winkle began a campaign of breaking in upon the assembly, taunting all present, sparing none, including Nicholas Vedder himself, whom she charged outright with encouraging her husband in habits of idleness.

Poor Rip! Now, to escape from the labor of the farm and clamor of his wife, his only alternative was to take his fowling piece and stroll away to the woods for a hunt. On these outings he would seat himself at the foot of a tree and share morsels of bread and cheese with Wolf, his fellow sufferer. "Poor Wolf," he would say, "thy mistress has made a dog's life of it, but never mind, my lad, while I live you shall not want for a friend!" Wolf would wag his tail, look wistfully into his master's face, and if a dog can feel pity, I believe Wolf did.

It was on a long ramble of this very kind, one fine autumn day, when Rip unconsciously scrambled to one of the highest parts of the Catskill Mountains. He was after his favorite sport of squirrel shooting, and the still quiet of the mountains echoed with the blast of his gun.

Late in the afternoon, panting and fatigued, he threw himself down on a grassy, flowered knoll that formed the crest of a lofty mountain. From his perch he could see the lordly Hudson, moving on a silent, majestic course far, far below him. Turning in the opposite direction, Rip peered down into a deep mountain glen, wild, lonely, and filled with fragments from the looming rock cliffs. For some time, Rip lay musing on this scene, but evening was gradually advancing and the mountains had begun to cast their long blue shadows. Rip, rising, and just about to begin his descent from the highlands, gave a heavy sigh, knowing that Dame Van Winkle would be waiting for him.

Suddenly he heard a voice from a distance, hallooing, "Rip Van Winkle! Rip Van Winkle!" He looked around and saw nothing but a crow winging on its solitary flight across the mountain. He thought his ears must have tricked him. He turned again to descend, when he heard the same cry ring through the evening air: "Rip Van Winkle! Rip Van Winkle!" At this Wolf bristled, and giving a large growl, he skulked to his master's side and looked fearfully down into the glen.

Rip, too, felt a twinge of apprehension as he looked anxiously in the same direction. Through the gloom Rip perceived a strange figure who appeared bent over, under the weight of something he carried on his back, slowly climbing up the rocks. Rip was surprised to see any human being in this lonely place, but supposing it to be some traveler in need of his assistance, he hastened down to greet the stranger.

Upon approaching, he was still more surprised at the stranger's appearance. He was a short, square-built old fellow, with thick, bushy hair and a grizzled beard. His clothes were of antique Dutch fashion: a cloth jerkin

around the waist and britches of ample volume decorated with rows of buttons down the sides and gathered into bunches at the knees. He bore on his shoulder a stout wooden keg, which, by the effort of the man's labor, Rip supposed to be full.

The stranger made signs for Rip to approach and assist him with the load. Though rather shy and distrustful of this new acquaintance, Rip complied with his usual good spirit. The pair clambered up a narrow, rocky gully, helping each other with the keg as they climbed. Every so often Rip could hear long, rolling rumbles, like distant thunder, which seemed to come from a deep ravine located between two lofty rocks and into which their rugged path led. He paused for an instant to listen, supposing it was the muttering of one of those occasional thundershowers that often take place in mountain heights.

Rip and his companion proceeded, passing through the gap in the rocks, whereupon they came to a natural hollow, much like a small amphitheater, surrounded by steep rock walls. Laboring in silence throughout the climb, Rip had deeply wondered what the point of carrying a heavy keg of spirits up this wild mountain could be. Yet there was something irresistible about the unknown that inspired his curiosity and stunted his better judgment!

As Rip entered the amphitheater, amazing sights suddenly presented themselves to him. There, on a level spot in the center, was a company of odd-looking fellows playing a game of ninepins, dressed in outlandish costumes: some wore short doublets, others jerkins, with long knives in their belts, and most of them had enormous britches, similar in style to those worn by Rip's companion. Their expressions, too, were peculiar; one had a large beard, broad face, and small piggish eyes. The face of another seemed to consist entirely of nose, and was surmounted by a white sugar-loaf hat, set off with a little rooster tail. There was one, however, who seemed to be the commander. He was a stout old gentleman with a weather-beaten expression who wore a laced doublet, broad belt and hanger, high-crowned hat with feather, red stockings, and high-heeled shoes with roses on them. The entire group reminded Rip of figures in an old Dutch painting he had once seen.

What seemed most strange to Rip was that, while these fellows were evidently amusing themselves, not one said a word. They were, thought Rip, the gloomiest party of pleasure seekers he had ever seen! Nothing interrupted the stillness of the scene but the noise of the ninepin balls, which, whenever they were rolled, echoed along the mountains like great rumbling peals of thunder.

As Rip and his companion approached the men, they suddenly quit their play and looked at him with such strange, crude expressions that his heart turned within him and his knees knocked together. His companion emptied the liquid contents of the keg into large flagons, and signaled for Rip to wait upon the men. Trembling with fear, Rip quickly served them. Whereupon they quaffed their drink in profound silence and then returned to their game.

Gradually Rip's amazement and fear eased, and when no one was watching he even ventured to taste the drink, which he found had much

flavor and suited him well. After the hard labors of the day, he was naturally a thirsty soul and soon was tempted to refill his flagon and repeat the experience. One taste provoked another, and soon his senses were overpowered by the drink. Whereupon Rip's eyes rolled back, his head gradually declined, and he fell into a deep sleep.

Waking, he found himself on the green knoll where he had first seen the old man of the glen. Rip rubbed his eyes; it was a bright sunny morning. The birds were hopping and twittering among the bushes, and an eagle was wheeling aloft. Breathing in the pure mountain breeze, Rip thought, *Surely I have not slept here all night.* He recalled the events before he had fallen asleep: the strange man with a keg of spirits, the mountain ravine, the wild retreat among the rocks, the woebegone party playing at ninepins, the flagon. *Oh! that wicked flagon! That wicked flagon!* thought Rip. *What excuse shall I make to Dame Van Winkle?*

He looked around for his gun, but in place of the clean, well-oiled fowling piece, he found an old firelock lying by him, the barrels encrusted with rust, the lock falling off, and the stock worm-eaten. He suspected that the mysterious men of the mountains had played a trick upon him, dosing him with drink, then robbing him of his own gun. Wolf, too, had disappeared, but perhaps he might have strayed after a squirrel or a partridge. Rip whistled for him and shouted his name, but all to no avail. The echoes repeated his whistle and shouts, but no dog was to be seen.

He determined to revisit the scene of last evening's event and, if he met with any of that strange party, to demand his dog and gun. As he rose to walk, he found himself stiff in the joints, and slow to get moving. *These mountain beds do not agree with me,* thought Rip. *And if this frolic should lay me up with rheumatism, what will Dame Van Winkle say?*

With some difficulty he climbed down into the glen, where he soon found the gully that he and his companion had traveled the preceding evening.

To his astonishment, a mountain stream was now foaming down it, leaping from rock to rock and filling the glen with babbling murmurs. Rip, forced to scramble up its sides, worked his way through witch hazel and thickets of birch, frequently tripping in the tangle of wild grapevines that twisted their coils from tree to tree.

Eventually he reached the spot where the ravine had formed an entrance through the cliffs to the amphitheater. Now, though, no trace of such an opening remained! The rocks presented a high, solid wall over which a torrent of water came tumbling in a sheet of feathery foam. Here, then, poor Rip was brought to a standstill.

He again called and whistled for Wolf, only to be answered by the caw-ing of a flock of crows, sporting about high in the air. What was to be done? The morning was passing away, and Rip was starving for want of his break-fast. He grieved to give up his dog and gun, and he dreaded to meet his wife, but it would not do to starve among the mountains. He shook his head, shoul-dered the rusty gun, and with a heart full of trouble and anxiety, turned his steps homeward.

As he approached the village he met a number of people, but not a one whom he knew, which surprised him, for he had thought himself acquainted with everyone in the county. And all those he encountered stared at him with equal surprise. Whenever they cast their eyes upon him, they invariably

stroked their chins and made mention of his amazing whiskers. Confused at first, Rip stroked his own chin and, to his astonishment, found his beard had grown to be more than a foot long!

When he entered the village, a troop of unfamiliar children ran at his heels, hooting after him, and pointing at his long gray beard. The dogs, too, none of which he recognized, barked at him as he passed. The village had changed. It was larger and there were many more people. There were rows of houses he had never seen before, and those which had been his familiar haunts were gone. Strange names were over the doors, strange faces were at the windows—everything was strange.

He began to wonder whether he and the world around him were bewitched.

Surely this was his native village, the one he had left only the day before. There stood the Catskill Mountains, there ran the silvery Hudson. At a distance were every hill and dale, precisely where they always had been. Rip was sorely perplexed: *That flagon last night,* thought he, *has confused my poor head!*

It was with some difficulty that he eventually found his way to his own house, expecting with every step to hear the angry voice of Dame Van Winkle. He found the house a shambles. The roof had fallen in, the windows were shattered, and the doors swung from their hinges. A half-starved dog that looked like Wolf was skulking about, and Rip called him by name, but the beast snarled, showed his teeth and ran off. "My very dog," sighed poor Rip, "has forgotten me!"

He entered the house. It was empty, forlorn, and apparently abandoned. He called aloud for his wife and children. The lonely rooms rang for a moment with his voice, and then all was silent.

He now hurried to his old resort, the village inn, but it, too, was gone. A large yellow wooden building stood in its place, with great gaping windows and a massive porch. Over the door was painted THE UNION HOTEL, BY JONATHAN DOOLITTLE. Near the great tree under which he had spent many a happy hour, there now rose a tall, naked pole with something on the top that looked like a red nightcap, and from it was fluttering a flag, on which was a peculiar arrangment of stars and stripes.

He did, however, recognize the sign with the ruby face of King George, under which he had smoked so many a peaceful pipe, but even this was oddly different. The red coat was changed for one of blue and buff, a sword instead of a scepter was held in the hand, the head was decorated with a cocked hat, and underneath was painted in large letters GENERAL WASHINGTON!

There was, as usual, a crowd of folks about the door, but none that Rip remembered. The very character of these people seemed changed. Every one of them was busy and bustling. Gone were the drowsy tranquility and friendship he remembered so well. He looked for the sage Nicholas Vedder, with his broad face, double chin, and long pipe, uttering clouds of tobacco smoke. And for Van Bummel, the schoolmaster, whom he might have expected to hear doling out the contents of an ancient newspaper. In place of these men was a lean, cranky-looking fellow, with his pockets full of political handbills. He was extolling on the rights of citizens, liberty and the victory at Bunker Hill, the heroes of 'seventy-six—on and on he went. This was all a perfect gibberish to the bewildered Rip.

The appearance of Rip, with his long grizzled beard, his rusty shotgun, his crude dress, and an army of women and children at his heels, soon attracted the attention of the tavern politicians. They crowded around him, eyeing him from head to foot with great curiosity. The lean and cranky speaker bustled up to him and, drawing Rip aside, inquired, "On which side do you vote?" Another short, busy little fellow pulled him by the arm and, rising on tiptoes, inquired in his ear, "Are you a Federal or a Democrat?"

Rip was equally at a loss to understand both of these questions, for he had no idea of what they were talking. Suddenly a knowing, self-important old gentleman in a sharply cocked hat made his way through the crowd, shoving people to the right and to the left with his elbows. Planting himself next to Rip, with one hand on his hip, the other on his cane, and with his keen eyes penetrating into Rip's very soul, he demanded in a severe tone, "What has brought you to the election with a gun on your shoulder and a mob at your heels? Is it your intention to start a riot in this village?"

"Alas, gentlemen," cried Rip, "I am a poor, quiet man, a native of the place, and a loyal subject of the king, God bless him!"

This last remark brought a hail of loud shouts from the bystanders: "A Tory! A Tory! A spy! A fugitive! Hustle him away to the jail!" With great difficulty the man in the cocked hat restored order. With an expression now tenfold more serious than before, he again demanded of Rip why he had come there, and whom he was seeking! Poor Rip humbly assured the man that he merely came there in search of some of his neighbors, who used to keep company about the tavern. "Well who are they? Name them." Rip thought for a moment, and inquired, "Where is Nicholas Vedder, the innkeeper?"

There was a silence until an old man replied, in a thin, piping voice, "Nicholas Vedder! Why, he is dead and gone these eighteen years!"

"Where's Brom Dutcher?"

"Oh, he went off to the army at the beginning of the war. Some say he was killed at the battle for Stony Point."

"Where's Van Bummel, the schoolmaster?"

"He went off to the wars, too, became a great general, and is now in Congress."

Rip's heart sank on hearing of these sad changes, for it seemed to him that he was now alone in the world. He was puzzled, too! Every answer from the crowd made no sense to him: What war? What Congress? What battle at Stony Point? Rip had no courage to ask after other friends, but cried out in despair, "Does anybody here know Rip Van Winkle?"

"Oh, Rip Van Winkle!" exclaimed two or three. "Oh, to be sure! That's Rip Van Winkle yonder, leaning against the tree."

Rip looked and beheld a precise twin of himself, just as he had appeared the day he went up the mountain. Poor Rip. Was he himself or another man?

In the midst of this bewilderment, the man in the cocked hat demanded to know who Rip was, and his name.

"God knows," exclaimed Rip, now at his wit's end. "I'm not myself—I'm somebody else—that's me yonder—no—that's somebody else who has got into my shoes—I was myself last night, but I fell asleep on the mountain, they've changed my gun, everything's changed, I'm changed, and I can't tell what my name is or who I am!"

At this, some of the bystanders cast knowing looks at one another, and a few tapped their fingers against their skulls, indicating that this strange fellow was certainly mad. Someone whispered that they should secure Rip's gun and keep the old fellow from doing any mischief.

Just at this critical moment, a bright and comely woman pressed through the throng to get a peep at the gray-bearded man who was causing the commotion. In her arms she had a chubby child, who was frightened at the bearded man's looks and began to cry.

"Hush, Rip," cried she, "hush now, the old man won't hurt you."

The name of the child, the manner of the mother, and the tone of her voice all awakened a train of recollections in old Rip's mind.

"What is your name, my good woman?" he asked.

"Judith Gardenier."

"And your father's name?"

"Ah, that poor man, Rip Van Winkle was his name, but it's twenty years since he went away from home with his gun, and never has been heard of since. His dog came home without him, but whether by chance he shot himself or was carried away by the Indians, nobody can tell."

Rip had but one more question to ask, and he put it to her with a faltering voice: "Where's your mother?"

"Oh, she, too, died but a short time ago; she broke a blood vessel in a fit of anger, haggling with a traveling peddler."

"Indeed that is tragic news," said Rip as he rushed toward the woman, catching her up in his arms. He could contain himself no longer.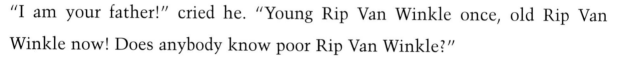

"I am your father!" cried he. "Young Rip Van Winkle once, old Rip Van Winkle now! Does anybody know poor Rip Van Winkle?"

All stood amazed until an old woman, tottering out from among the crowd, put her hand to her brow, peered into his face, and after a moment exclaimed, "Sure enough! It is Rip Van Winkle—it is himself! Welcome home again, old neighbor. Why, where have you been these twenty long years?"

Rip's story was soon told; twenty years had been to Rip but one long night's sleep. The neighbors stared in disbelief when they heard it, and some were seen to wink in doubt, while others worked to contain bursts of laughter, for most thought Rip was playing an elaborate prank on them. The self-important man in the cocked hat looked at Rip, and shook his head in disbelief.

It was determined, however, to take the opinion of old Peter Vanderdonk, the most ancient inhabitant of the village, who was slowly advancing up the road. Peter was well versed in all the wonderful events and traditions of the neighborhood. He remembered Rip at once, and corroborated his story in a most satisfactory manner. He assured the citizens that it was a fact, handed down from his ancestors, famous for their historical knowledge, that the Catskill Mountains had always been haunted by strange beings. Old Peter said, "The spirit of the great Hendrick Hudson himself, the famous explorer for whom the river was named, keeps a kind of vigil in those mountains every twenty years. Along with his crew from his ship, *Half Moon*, he revisits the scene of his famous exploration, keeping a guardian eye over the river." Old Peter told of how his own father had once seen those strange men in their old Dutch outfits playing ninepins in a hollow of the mountain and that he himself had heard, one summer afternoon, the sound of their rumbling balls echoing like distant peals of thunder.

Upon hearing Old Peter's story there was little more the crowd could say or do, so still shaking their heads in wonderment, the townspeople returned to the more important concerns of the election.

Rip's daughter took him home to live with her. She had a snug, well-furnished house, and a stout, happy farmer for a husband. Rip remembered him to be one of the urchins who used to climb on his back in younger days. As for Rip's son, he, too, lived on his sister's farm, where he loafed away time, and was thought by most folks to be the laziest man in the county.

Old Rip resumed his old walks and habits and soon found many of his former cronies, though all were rather worse for the wear and tear of time.

With little to do at home and having arrived at that happy age when a man can be idle without guilt, he took his place once more on the bench near the inn door. Soon he was revered by all as a village patriarch and historian of the old times "before the Revolutionary War." And, as you might expect, Rip carried on in his old age much as he had in his younger days. He didn't fret over the past, and once again took life just as it came. He kept his whiskers, and before long he had a new dog, who was without question the rightful heir to Wolf.

Rip would tell his story to every stranger who arrived at Doolittle's Hotel and was willing to listen. There was not a man, woman, or child in the neighborhood who did not come to know it. Some always claimed to doubt the reality of it, and insisted that Rip had been out of his head. The old Dutch inhabitants of these parts, however, universally gave it full credit. Even to this day, they never hear a summer thunderstorm rumbling in the Catskill peaks, but what they say, "Hendrick Hudson and his crew are playing at their game of ninepins!"

WASHINGTON IRVING (1783-1859) was an author and diplomat well known for his essays, stories, and satirical pieces. Born in New York City, Irving began his literary career by writing about New York society and the theater. After an unsuccessful attempt to save a branch of his family's hardware store in 1815, Irving began writing full-time. His stories "Rip Van Winkle" and "The Legend of Sleepy Hollow," published in 1820, made him world famous as a writer.

WILL MOSES began painting at the age of four with his grandfather, Forrest K. Moses, a folk artist who learned to paint from his mother, Anna Mary Robertson, better known as Grandma Moses. Will has received world-wide recognition for his individual folk style, and his art has been displayed in some of the nation's most prestigious collections, including the Smithsonian Institution and the White House.

Will Moses works out of his studio at the Mount Nebo Gallery and Farm in Eagle Bridge, New York, where he lives with his wife, Sharon, their two sons, and a daughter.